# Emily and the Ostriches

Written by Dan Bernstein

Illustrated by Gary Aagaard

RIZZOLI
NEW YORK

First published in the United States of America in 1995
by Rizzoli International Publications, Inc.
300 Park Avenue South, New York, New York, 10010

Library of Congress Cataloging-in-Publications Data
Bernstein, Dan.
Emily and the ostriches / written by Dan Bernstein;
illustrated by Gary Aagaard
p.    cm.
Summary: Emily, a dazzling young ballerina, is magically
transported to Ostrichville, where, in spite of her strangeness, she is
eventually accepted by the birds and perfects her ballet technique.
ISBN  0-8478-1917-5
[1. Ostriches—Fiction. 2. Ballet dancing—Fiction.]  I. Aagaard, Gary, ill.
II. Title.
PZ7.B4565E   1995
[E]—dc20                              95-6844
CIP    AC

Designed by Barbara Balch
Printed and bound in Singapore

For Krista Kennedy McNamara

And, to Kelly and all the O'haras, Sophie, Candia, Gerry, Karen, and hundreds of Riverside, California, elementary school students who listened and laughed and offered their honest comments and suggestions, thanks.

Emily was a dazzling young ballerina who loved to dance so much that she never walked or ran or rode anywhere. She danced.

She danced to school in long, leaping strides, especially when she was running—or dancing—late. She danced home from the store, sometimes twirling long, pink swirls of toilet paper over her head, although every time she did this, she got into big trouble with her mom.

One cold, snowy winter day, Emily had to stay cooped up inside all morning and almost all afternoon. She had never gone that long without dancing.

*"Please,"* she begged her mother, *"can't I just dance to the corner?"* At first, Emily's mother said no. Then she said no again. And again. And again. In addition to being a dazzling ballerina, Emily could be a big pest.

Finally, Emily's mother gave in. *"Okay,"* she said. *"You may dance to the corner and back. But no further. And leave the toilet paper in the bathroom."*

So, dressed only in her brightest ballerina dress and her newest ballet shoes, Emily danced out into the blizzard. And disappeared. No one knows quite how it happened. Some say the blizzard was so thick that Emily just got lost. Others say Emily was so full of energy after spending the whole day in the house that she leaped and loped and twirled and pirouetted like never before. And she may actually have become part of the blizzard, though she would have made an unusually large snowflake.

But everybody agreed on one thing: Emily, the dazzling ballerina, had vanished.

$\mathcal{W}$hat they didn't know was that Emily was perfectly all right.
That is, if a dazzling ballerina can be perfectly all right when she
winds up in a village populated entirely by ostriches.

Emily's blizzard ballet had carried her down the street, past
the corner, and into a glittery, powdery passageway that melted
magically into Ostrichville (population: 300).

*"Wait until they hear about this back home!"* Emily exclaimed, a little nervously. The truth was, Emily had no idea how to get back home. She couldn't figure out how a simple dance to the corner had swept and swirled her to such an unusual place. She had no idea how to dance her way out. And the ostriches were absolutely no help at all.

*E*very time she approached them and asked in her friendliest voice, *"Please, could you show me the way home?"* they would smirk little ostrich smirks and bury their heads in the soft Ostrichville soil.

The ostriches were not very nice to Emily. They had never seen anything like her before.

*"Look at her!"* cackled Barry, the village loudmouth. *"She doesn't even have a neck!"*

*"Yeah!"* croaked Hilda, the best dancing ostrich in Ostrichville. *"And look at those things popping out of her shoulders. She calls them arms! Who needs arms?"*

*"Well,"* noted Ernest, the youngest and quietest ostrich in the village, *"she doesn't have a beak. Maybe arms come in handy."*

*"Look,"* snapped Barry, curling his beak into an ugly sneer. *"She's not one of us. No neck, no beak, two arms, one freak!"*

All the ostriches, except Ernest, took up the chant: *"No neck, no beak, two arms, one freak! No neck, no beak, two arms, one freak!"*

Emily knew what the ostriches were saying about her, and it made her sad. But there wasn't anything she could do. She couldn't grow a neck or a beak, and she actually found her arms quite useful. But, living among the ostriches, she felt so different from everyone else.

Not every ostrich was mean to Emily. Ernest's parents, Herman and Florence, were so taken with the dazzling ballerina that they invited her to live with them. Emily, of course, would have preferred to be back home with her real parents. She missed them terribly. But she was very happy to move in with Ernest and his parents, who said nothing about her arms or hair or ears or even her short neck and missing beak. All Herman and Florence said was: *"Emily, we are very pleased that you've decided to live with us. We expect you to clean up your room and, of course, being ostriches, we never eat eggs."*

Ernest was thrilled to have a sister, especially one as beautiful and graceful as Emily. Each morning, after they had cleaned up their rooms, Ernest and Emily would dash through the village, leaping and loping, sprinting, springing, and very nearly soaring through Ostrichville Square and out into the countryside, where ostrich speed limits were rarely enforced.

The other ostriches sniggered and giggled and chortled as Ernest and Emily sailed by. They gossiped and spread rumors that Emily was neither human nor ostrich, nothing but a goofy ballerina bird who, once hatched, had been abandoned by her shocked and embarrassed parents.

However, even these loose-beaked birds couldn't help noticing that, day after day, Emily seemed to be leaping farther and farther and running faster and faster, and doing both with an easy gracefulness that not even Hilda, their best dancer, could match.

$S$*he's definitely got the moves,"* marveled Barry, the loudmouth of Ostrichville.

*"I couldn't do that even if I did have arms,"* pouted Hilda. Gradually, something strange happened. At first the ostriches just got used to having Emily around. Then, they almost seemed to forget about her arms and her tiny neck and her un-beak-like lips. Barry stopped teasing Emily. And Hilda and Emily even worked together on a dance routine for the annual village talent show.

As the days stretched into weeks, Emily and the ostriches realized they had a lot in common. They loved to run. They loved to dance. They didn't eat eggs. And they really hated cleaning up their rooms, even though their parents made them do it anyway.

Emily was very happy in Ostrichville, but when she thought of her real parents, she became sad. She often danced through Ostrichville Square and out into the countryside, searching for the magical passageway she had entered during her ballet into the blizzard.

One day, as Emily danced and leaped over the countryside, she felt something very strange. She felt as if she was being watched. Emily was not afraid. Just curious. So she allowed herself to glide toward a thick stand of trees. As she got closer and closer, Emily thought she saw a little bird of a man peering out at her. He seemed to be watching her from another world. Emily was so startled to see such an un-ostrich-like creature that she raced back to Ostrichville Square to warn the others.

Just as she was getting to the good part, *"He doesn't have a neck and he doesn't have a beak!"* the little man himself fluttered into view.

"Hubert G. Starling at your service," he said with a slight bow. "I don't suppose you've heard of me."

"Why no!" exclaimed Emily. "I don't suppose we have!"

"No matter," he smiled. "You've probably heard of the Big Apple Ballet. I make up the dances. I get my ideas from the ostriches. Been watching them for years. Been watching you, young lady, for weeks. I'd like you to dance in my ballet."

Well, you can imagine the commotion! The ostriches were delighted that Hubert G. Starling had been using them as models for his dances. And they were proud that Emily had been asked to dance with the Big Apple Ballet. They even decided to accompany her to New York City—as long as they got free tickets to the show. After all, Emily would never have been discovered if she hadn't come to Ostrichville.

Only Emily was confused. "But Mr. Starling," she said, "there's no way out of Ostrichville. I've looked and looked."

Hubert G. Starling smiled and took her tiny hand. "There was a way in. There is a way out. Just follow me." And so Emily left Ostrichville just as magically and mysteriously as she had gotten there.

$\mathcal{T}$he night of Emily's big performance, all of New York's glittering finest filed into the large hall. The proud, glittery ostriches filed in right along with them. Herman, Florence, and Ernest sat in a special box. Barry, Hilda, and the others eased their freshly washed feathers into plush first row seats.

But before Barry and Hilda could turn to the glittering New Yorkers and boast that Emily, the dazzling ballerina, belonged to

Ostrichville, loud whispers reached them first. *"Hey, look at those noodle necks!"* *"Get a load of those ridiculous clothes!"* *"How do they expect us to see around those silly hats?"* *"Hey, what is this—a ballet or a circus?"*

Barry, Hilda, and the other ostriches were stunned and hurt. How could people be so cruel? Why couldn't people be more like ostriches?

When the curtain opened, out danced Emily. She danced and she dazzled. She leaped and twirled with power and grace that even the ostriches had never seen. She dazzled the glittery New Yorkers. She even dazzled the critics. But, most of all, she dazzled her real parents, who had come to New York City after reading about *"Emily—The Ballerina Raised By Ostriches!"* They had hoped it would be her. They had almost given up hope of ever seeing her again, but when they arrived at the theater and saw the big ballet posters, they knew it was their Emily.

Emily was so happy to see her real parents again that she decided to go home with them. She wasn't ready for a career as a ballerina—at least not yet—and while she had grown quite fond of Ostrichville, she didn't really want to live there.

Emily kept dancing, day in and day out. Not running, walking, or riding. Just dancing. And yes, sometimes even twirling toilet paper.

Eventually, she and Ernest formed the Ballerina–Ostrich Troupe. They danced in New York. They danced in Ostrichville. They danced and dazzled, proudly displaying their necks and beaks and arms and wings and hair and feathers everywhere they went.

But they didn't dance in blizzards. And they didn't eat eggs.